Just add
water!

No Ordinary Girl

Read other titles in the series

h2o
Just add water!

1 No Ordinary Girl

2 Living With Secrets

3 Fishy Business (Coming Soon)

No Ordinary Girl

Adapted by Rachel Elliot

SIMON AND SCHUSTER

SIMON AND SCHUSTER
First published in Great Britain in 2009 by Simon & Schuster UK Ltd,
1st Floor, 222 Gray's Inn Road, London WC1X 8HB
A CBS Company

Originally published in Australia in 2007 by Parragon

A CIP catalogue record for this book is available from the British Library

ISBN 978-1-84738-487-4

10 9 8 7 6 5 4 3 2 1

Printed by CPI Cox & Wyman, Reading, Berkshire RG1 8EX

 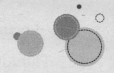

Emma Gilbert dived into the pool with barely a splash, and then curved up to the surface. Her hands carved through the water – each clean stroke followed by another executed just as skilfully. She concentrated on keeping her breathing steady and her movements controlled, enjoying the feeling of the water rippling over her arms. Her long blonde hair was packed tightly into a close-fitting swimming cap to keep her as streamlined as possible. *Speed and control*, she said to herself over and over again. *Speed and control*. That's what would help her win the regional swimming championships one day.

On the side of the pool, her best friend, Cleo Sertori, watched in admiration. Emma's strokes cut through the shimmering surface of the water without making a single splash. She looked as if

she'd been swimming her entire life.

Thinking about it, Cleo realized that really it wasn't all too far from the truth. Emma had been swimming since she was six months old, and for all the years Cleo had known her, it had been her friend's greatest passion. Cleo couldn't swim a single stroke, but she still got a lot of fun out of helping Emma to train. At first, Emma had tried to persuade Cleo to join her. But as much as Cleo loved watching her friend swim, she hated the idea of getting into the water herself. The very thought of it made her feel sick.

With one final kick, Emma glided up to the edge of the pool and pulled off her goggles as Cleo quickly hit the stopwatch. She leant down beside the pool to show Emma her time, and Emma's face lit up with a smile.

"Awesome, that's point two under my personal best," she said, looking at the display.

"Emma, you were really motoring then," said Cleo.

Emma smiled up at her friend. She really appreciated Cleo's help while she was training. It was way more fun to have someone there with her, encouraging her on.

"I'll do better than that tomorrow," she said. "Give me two weeks and I'll be ready for the regionals."

She looked full of excitement and enthusiasm. Cleo suddenly wished that she had something that made her feel like that. Pushing the thought aside, she beamed down at Emma, who was getting ready for another lap.

"It's *so* cool," she said.

Emma smiled in agreement, and then put her goggles back on and launched off from the side of the pool. Cleo looked down at the stopwatch again, thinking how exciting it would be to watch her best friend take part in the regional competition. She had no doubt that Emma would win. Emma could do anything she set her mind to.

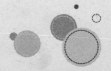

After Emma had finished training for the day, the girls agreed to meet up at the Juice-Net Café later on. Emma had to go home and get changed, and Cleo really needed to put in some time studying biology. They arranged a meeting time and then headed off in different directions.

It was a hot day and Cleo decided to walk home around the marina. She enjoyed the cool breeze that came off the water, and was soon lost in thought. She was picturing Emma's look of enthusiasm and hope. Emma was so incredibly talented. Not only that, she was dedicated as well. It wasn't just luck that had taken her so far, but a lot of very hard work. Emma was totally focused on her dream of becoming a champion swimmer, and she was getting closer and closer to making that dream a reality.

Of course, Cleo knew how much Emma loved swimming, so it can't seem like work to her. But Cleo appreciated what Emma put into it and she was happy to do anything she could to

4

help her best friend. It was just … Cleo let out a long sigh. She wondered how it would feel to have a dream like Emma – to have such ambition. Now that the girls were nearly sixteen, it sometimes seemed as if everyone except her had found something they were passionate about.

Cleo shrugged off the thought. There was plenty of time. And right then things were super busy as it was.

She was worrying about all the biology studying she had to catch up on when she heard a deep voice.

"Cleo!"

Cleo looked up and gaped. Zane Bennett was calling to her from one of the berths – no doubt where one of his dad's yachts was kept.

Zane Bennett was an arrogant jerk. He had always thought he could get away with anything because his dad was rich. In fact, his dad was the only person more obnoxious than him.

Zane had a screwdriver in his hand and that permanent look of arrogance on his face. He was crouching on the side of the marina, next to his little boat. The engine cover was off and it looked as if he was having trouble. Cleo let out a sigh and hoped that he wasn't talking to her. He had certainly never bothered with her before, and it wasn't as if she knew anything about boats. She was surprised he even knew her name. She put her head down and kept walking.

"Hey! Cleo!" he called again.

It was no use ignoring him; he knew she'd seen him. She looked over, cautiously, still hoping that he might have been talking to someone else.

"Yes, *that* Cleo," he said with an easy laugh.

Cleo was confused – he sounded almost *friendly*.

"I'm in some trouble here, can you help?" he asked.

He stood up and looked at her, his blue eyes looking soft and pleading.

Cleo hesitated. "Er, I don't think so," she said, backing away.

"C'mon. *Please?*" He really sounded sincere. "My Zodiac won't go. And all I need you to do is just pass me the tools."

He looked at the small boat in front of him – the Zodiac – and really did look like he needed a hand. Cleo rolled her eyes, flicked back her long, dark plait and started walking towards him.

Arrogant and incredibly annoying he might be, but if he's in real trouble and needs a hand, I can't really refuse, can I? she thought as she walked behind him and looked down into the boat.

"I'm not good with boats," she told him, stepping down into the Zodiac. It swayed under her weight and she clutched hold of the wheel, feeling reluctant and very uneasy.

"You'll be fine," said Zane with confidence. His voice was gentle and encouraging. Cleo had never heard Zane Bennett sound like that before.

That should have warned her.

Cleo wasn't looking at Zane – she was concentrating on not losing her balance and falling into the water. If she had glanced behind her, she would have seen that he was silently untying the mooring rope.

"It took me a while to realize that someone stole my spark plug," he continued in that same, gentle voice.

"So, does it work without one?" Cleo asked, trying to show an interest and take her mind off the fact that she was *on the water*. She picked a few tools out of the toolbox on board, wondering which ones he would need.

"Nah," Zane laughed, his voice harsh and cruel. "No spark plug, no spark!"

Then Cleo felt the boat lurch beneath her

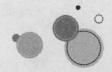

and turned to see Zane's foot push against the hull. The Zodiac shot out into the marina. Cleo was adrift without an engine, and she was heading out to sea!

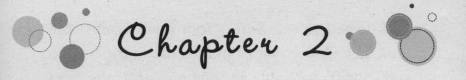

Chapter 2

Cleo felt her heart leap into her throat. She tried to stay still, but she was shaking with fear and anger – mostly fear. She was terrified of the water. Even though she had grown up by the sea, she had never learned to swim, and her worst nightmares always involved being adrift at sea with no hope of rescue. Now it looked as though they were coming true.

Zane laughed as he stood on the marina deck, watching Cleo float away. His friend Nate appeared from behind one of the larger boats, where he'd been hiding, and they sniggered as Cleo and the Zodiac drifted further and further from them, its rope trailing in the water.

"I was getting sick of that thing anyway," he said, as Nate grinned at him.

"Why *me*?" Cleo shouted back, drifting further out with every word. "*I* didn't steal your

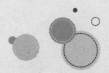

spark plug."

"Because you're *here*, Cleo," Zane said, as if it was the most obvious reason in the world.

His face darkened into a frown. When he had found that his boat wouldn't work, all he had wanted was a scapegoat to blame. Then, just at the right moment, little Cleo Sertori had appeared. Making someone else suffer always made Zane feel better.

"My dad'll buy me another boat anyway," he called to her. "I'll tell you what, if you get it going, you can keep it."

"This isn't funny!" Cleo shouted, angrily. *Don't they realize how dangerous this is?* she thought. *I have no idea how to control this thing, and I'm heading out to sea!*

"Are you kidding?" Zane chuckled. "Works for me, right Nate?"

The two boys high-fived each other and cracked up. They both got a buzz from seeing Cleo's frightened face. Nate gave Cleo a little

wave as the boat moved further and further out of the marina.

"Zane!" Cleo cried, but she knew that it was no use. There was no way that Zane Bennett was going to do a single thing to help her. *I don't know what I am supposed to do now*, she thought. *How can one person be so totally mean?*

"Looks like you'll have to swim for it, Cleo," Zane shouted.

He and Nate turned and left, nudging each other in the ribs and sniggering. Cleo heard their laughs growing fainter. Her eyes pricked with tears as she floated past jetties and boats. There was no one in sight – no one to call to for help. She didn't have her mobile with her, and no one knew that she had gone down to the marina – she hadn't told Emma which way she was walking home.

"This isn't happening," she muttered. *What am I going to do?*

Cleo sat down carefully and leaned her chin on her hand. She stared back at the marina as

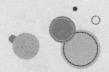

the figures of Zane and Nate grew smaller and smaller. The boat drifted further out, never getting close enough to the walkways or other boats for her to grab hold of anything and stop herself. She was too scared to even feel angry. She was stuck in a boat with no power, she had no one to help her and she was terrified of the water. Cleo wondered if things could possibly get any worse.

The boat passed the last little wooden jetty, heading for the open sea. Cleo was at a loss for what to do next. Then suddenly a figure came flying from the jetty! The boat lurched as the newcomer leapt into the boat. Cleo felt the Zodiac pitch beneath her and let out a terrified scream, clutching at the sides of the boat. Spinning around, she saw a girl staring mischievously back at her. She had curly blonde hair and piercing blue eyes, and Cleo recognized her at once. It was Rikki Chadwick, the new girl from school.

Cleo's heart was still hammering and she was suddenly furious with this new passenger. For a

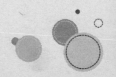

moment she had thought that Rikki could help her get back to dry land, but now she realized that wasn't going to happen.

"Is this supposed to be some sort of rescue?" she snapped. "Because there's a fatal flaw here. I don't mean to state the obvious, but we're just floating out to sea; *both* of us!"

Without answering, Rikki reached behind her back and produced a spark plug as if by magic. A smug smile flitted across her face.

"*You* took that!" Cleo stated. For a moment this suddenly all became Rikki's fault. Then she gave a little smile as she realized that the spark plug solved their problem. They had power! Rikki stepped past her towards the back of the boat.

"Zane Bennett's a pig," Rikki said as she grabbed a socket wrench from the bottom of the boat and replaced the spark plug. "Anything I can do to get under his skin can't be a bad thing, can it?"

Rikki glanced back over her shoulder to

where Zane and Nate were walking along. She had her own reasons for disliking Zane, and when she had seen his boat there, just *waiting* for someone to come along and mess with it … well … it had been too good an opportunity to miss.

As soon as she knew that they had power, Cleo's feeling of panic left her. Maybe this new girl wasn't so bad after all! Certainly anyone who could get one over on Zane Bennett was all right by her.

"Cool," she said with a smile. "Thanks, Rikki."

"You know my name?" Rikki asked, surprised.

"Yeah. Well, I've seen you around school, since you arrived," Cleo explained.

Rikki looked up at Cleo from the rear of the boat as she fitted the engine cover. She wore a strange expression, almost like a scowl, and suddenly Cleo realized that she must have seemed very rude. It must be horrible to be the

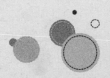

new girl and not have any friends.

"Oh, I mean I've *meant* to say hello and everything," Cleo said, trying to save the situation.

Rikki just raised an eyebrow, and Cleo got the feeling that she was digging herself a deeper hole. She stopped talking and just watched.

Having finished with the engine, Rikki turned the key in the ignition and started the boat. The engine roared to life. *Thank goodness for that!* Cleo thought. *This girl is awesome!*

"Hold on!" Rikki warned Cleo as she threw the throttle forward and the boat sped off.

The girls smiled at each other as Rikki turned the Zodiac around and steered it straight back to the marina. Zane and Nate were strolling along the walkway. Zane still had the screwdriver in his hand and was laughing. He stopped, standing like a model in a magazine, as if showing off his expensive clothes.

He really thinks he's hilarious, Rikki thought.

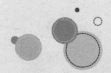

Well, we'll show him!

She aimed the boat directly at the boys and threw it into top gear. The Zodiac sped straight towards them, but at the last minute Rikki spun the wheel tightly and sent a wall of water arching towards the boys. It cascaded over Zane and Nate, but mostly over Zane. He lost his poise completely and crouched down, trying to protect himself from the water. But it was no use – Rikki's aim was deadly.

Zane's designer clothes were totally drenched and the smile had utterly vanished from his face. He could do nothing but scowl as Rikki and Cleo looked back over their shoulders at him, smiled and motored away. Nate couldn't stop giggling at the sight of Zane dripping wet and furious. Zane glared at Nate, who put his hand up to his mouth and tried to stifle his laughter. It was truly a sight for sore eyes.

I think I'm going to like this girl, Cleo thought.

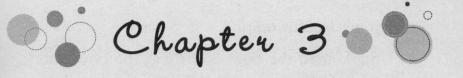

Chapter 3

Cleo glanced over at Rikki, who was steering the boat through the water with a blazing, determined look on her face. Cleo laughed out loud when she thought of Zane's expression as he was doused with water.

Rikki grinned at her and Cleo beamed back. Rikki tapped her on the shoulder and then pushed the throttle forward, as if daring Cleo to stop her. Ahead of them, the high-rise buildings of the city dominated the skyline as they motored down a canal.

"Yeah!" Cleo whooped.

Cleo and Rikki had the entire afternoon to spend tearing around the canals and along the shore in Zane's boat. After all, hadn't Zane said that Cleo could keep the Zodiac if she could get it going?

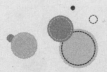

The girls sped over the water, waving to other boaters and enjoying the feeling of the salty air blowing back their hair. They zoomed along next to riverside cafés, shrieking with laughter. Rikki obviously knew about boats and the Zodiac responded to her slightest touch. She weaved around other boats and between any obstacles. Cleo was having a brilliant time, although she wished Rikki would slow down a bit.

This is excellent, she thought to herself as they cruised down one of the canals. *Rikki is so cool. I can't wait for Emma to meet her – I wonder if they'll like each other?* What had seemed like a disaster of a day had quickly turned into the most fun Cleo had had in ages. She smiled and allowed herself to imagine long summer days on the water with Rikki and Emma.

Emma was walking along the canal path on her way to meet Cleo at the Juice-Net Café. Her mind was taken up with thoughts of regionals and swimming championships. *One day I'm*

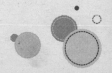

going to be swimming at the Olympics, she promised herself. *I know I can do it if I just keep focused!*

Her thoughts were interrupted by a buzzing sound that grew louder and louder. A red boat was powering along the canal – way too fast. *Idiots*, thought Emma, pursing up her lips. She thought she recognized Zane Bennett's boat and decided not to give him the satisfaction of looking his way. But then she heard a familiar voice.

"Hey Emma!" Cleo shouted. "Want a ride?"

Emma looked down and was astounded to see her friend in a boat. She gaped at Rikki for a moment, and then gathered her thoughts. *Of course, it's the new girl*, she remembered. *But what is she doing in Zane's boat? And how in the world did she persuade Cleo to get into it with her?*

"Are you licensed?" she shouted down to Rikki.

"Are you my mother?" Rikki called back

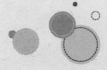

with a sarcastic smile, as she slowed down and drew in to the bank. This day was turning out better than she had expected. First she had brought Zane Bennett down a peg or two, and now she was actually making friends. *Maybe I'm gonna like it here after all*, she thought.

Emma hesitated for a moment, slightly irritated by Rikki's attitude. She didn't want to take any risks, but she knew that Cleo wouldn't be on board if Rikki was driving dangerously. A few minutes later she was climbing on board the Zodiac.

All afternoon, the three girls cruised the canals and shoreline in the Zodiac. Cleo told Emma about how Zane had tricked her, and even Emma laughed when she heard how Rikki had drenched him with water. It was about time someone showed him that he couldn't do whatever he wanted just because his dad was rich.

Cleo was happy. Although Rikki and Emma snapped at each other every now and then, they

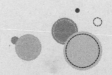

were mostly getting along well and all of them were having *the* coolest time. It was a great feeling, just the three of them on their own, not having to be anywhere and having the whole afternoon left to go wherever they felt like. Cleo thought that she could happily spend days powering up and down the canals.

Emma was feeling a little more cautious. From the short time she had known Rikki, she could tell that although she was smart, she was also a risk taker. *I mean*, thought Emma, *it sounds like she had to make quite a jump to get into the Zodiac earlier. Cleo would never have done that in a million years.* Emma looked over at her best friend and had to smile. She looked so happy – it was great to see her like that. Emma decided to forget her doubts and just focus on having fun.

However, Rikki was getting very bored with the same canals and scenery. She loved change and variety, and she could tell that neither of her new friends was likely to suggest anything more adventurous. *I guess it's up to me then*, she

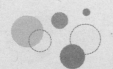
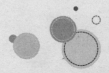

thought.

"Wanna go out to sea?" she suggested in her most casual voice. No big deal.

"Isn't it dangerous in a craft this size?" Emma asked immediately.

That girl is way too sensible for her own good, Rikki decided. *Someone needs to teach her how to loosen up a little!*

"Chill out," she said. Then she took charge of the situation before anyone else could argue with her, slammed the throttle forward and sped out of the marina into open water.

At first, they had the coolest time. Cruising around the canals had been fun, but seeing what the Zodiac could do on the open water was ten times better! The afternoon sun shone down on the water and made it gleam so brightly that the girls could hardly look at it. Cleo trailed her hand in the water as they sped through the blue waves, and Emma threw her head back,

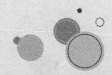

enjoying the feel of the warm, salty air in her hair. Rikki increased the speed and headed further out to sea, keen to show her new friends a good time. Since Rikki had moved to the Gold Coast, she had been pretty lonely. Now it looked as if Emma and Cleo might become good friends – even if they were a bit too cautious sometimes!

Then suddenly, Rikki felt the boat lurch under her control. The engine stuttered and spluttered. They slowed down and eventually stopped. Cleo looked at Emma in alarm as Rikki pressed the ignition switch. Nothing. She tried it over and over again, but she knew it was no good. They might have had the spark plug, but without petrol, the boat would do nothing but drift. They weren't going anywhere.

Cleo felt a cold shiver of fear run up and down her spine. They were stranded in the middle of the sea – it was as if her nightmares were coming true after all! She didn't even know if there were any life jackets on this boat. She tried to speak but her voice wouldn't work. She

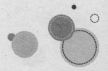

looked from Emma to Rikki and back to Emma again. What were they going to do?

Emma was glaring at Rikki, resting her chin on her fist in a mock-casual pose. Inside she was seething, but she knew that shouting wouldn't help the situation, so she was trying to keep her temper under control. She couldn't keep the sarcasm out of her voice, though.

"Are we chilled out yet?" she asked with a cold look.

Rikki bristled immediately. This girl was so uptight!

"So, we're floating," she answered back. "It's not like we're *sinking*."

"Not *yet*," Emma said, as if she thought they could be at any minute.

Rikki made a giant effort to control her own temper and ignored this dig. Cleo stared fearfully at the deep waters surrounding them. How were they going to get out of this?

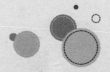

 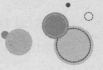

Chapter 4

"I think we're out of fuel," said Rikki, stating the obvious while she looked around them, searching for the nearest land.

Then she saw it. Straight ahead of them was a beautiful, mountainous island. Clouds drifted around its highest peaks, and its slopes were covered in lush green grass and trees. In the centre was a tall, rocky cone shape, almost like a volcano.

"Feel like paddling to that island?" she asked.

The reaction of the other two surprised her. They both looked horrified.

"Mako Island?" said Emma, giving a mirthless laugh. "Forget it."

It was typical of Rikki, she thought. *What a stupid suggestion!*

Rikki was looking at Emma for an explanation, but it was Cleo who spoke up.

"No one goes there," she said, finding her voice at last. "It's surrounded by sharks … and reefs … and mangroves."

Cleo's eyes opened wide as she thought of the many dangers that the island held. Her imagination was running riot. She pictured them all capsized and eaten by blood-crazed sharks. Emma glanced at her, knowing how melodramatic she must sound to someone who didn't know her.

Rikki couldn't see the problem. She reached down and picked up one of the oars.

"Well, it's all we've got," she said, as she handed Emma the oar.

Emma paused, and then realized that Rikki was right. With a sigh she took the oar and started paddling. Rikki picked up the other oar and paddled on the other side of the boat. Cleo stayed in between them, keeping her arms firmly inside the Zodiac and against her sides.

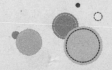

Who knew what sharks were capable of?

Rikki and Emma were both strong and they paddled hard. The boat drew closer and closer to Mako Island. They didn't need to paddle for long. They soon reached a sandy beach that was safe and out of the wind. It seemed like a good place to leave the boat while they thought of the best way back to the mainland. They dragged the Zodiac up the beach and looked up at the cliffs that towered above them.

"How are we ever going to get back home?" Cleo wondered aloud, as the waves thundered onto the shore behind her.

"Good question, Cleo," Emma replied, folding her arms and glaring at Rikki. "Ask your friend."

She was annoyed with Cleo for being in the boat with Rikki in the first place and annoyed at herself for agreeing to get into the boat with them, but most of all she was annoyed with Rikki for suggesting heading further out to sea.

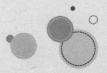

"Don't put this on me," snarled Rikki, who was beginning to wish she had never taken the stupid spark plug.

"Oh, it was someone *else's* fault?" Emma asked. "Someone *else* took this thing miles offshore?"

Rikki bit her lip and scowled as Emma reached into the boat for her bag. Cleo looked off into the distance. She hated arguments.

"You two are lucky I've got this," Emma said, pulling out her mobile phone and flipping it open.

She started to walk up and down the beach, looking down at her mobile. She turned on the spot in all directions and looked up and down the beach.

A smile of relief and delight spread over Cleo's face. They were going to be rescued. She leaned towards Rikki, trying to play the peacemaker.

"Emma's always *really* prepared," she said,

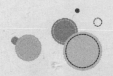

hoping that Rikki would see what a great friend Emma was.

"I'm so *happy* for her," Rikki replied, her voice dripping with sarcasm. She was in no mood to be nice.

Emma stopped and favoured Rikki with a glare.

"I'm not getting any signal," she said. "We should try and get to higher ground."

Cleo looked horrified and Rikki gave her a sidelong look. Emma began to walk towards the tree line, away from the beach, holding her phone up high and willing the signal bars to appear. Cleo glanced at Rikki and then followed Emma, but Rikki didn't move. She stayed still, leaning against the Zodiac and thinking.

Rikki didn't like the way Emma just gave orders and expected them to be followed. Cleo seemed happy to do whatever she was told, but that was no reason for Emma to think that she could boss everyone else around as well. On the other hand, finding higher ground *did* seem like

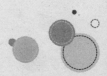

the most sensible idea. After a moment, Rikki let out a sigh and stomped off after the other two.

The three girls scrambled over the high boulders at the far end of the beach and clambered through long grasses. Soon they were walking along beside a still stream, pushing their way between jungly trees, leafy branches and creeping vines. It felt like a lost world. A faint mist hung over the water, and strange sounds filled the air. The trees were so tightly packed together that the sunlight filtered through in shafts of light, glistening on the surface of the streams that meandered across the island.

In some places the water was so still that the reflections of trees looked like the real thing, broken only by the occasional water creature coming up to the surface. Dense thickets of mangroves blocked their way and rare birds circled high overhead.

Rikki privately thought that there were

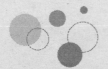

probably all sorts of poisonous snakes and spiders in the thick undergrowth, but she kept quiet about her ideas. She hadn't known Cleo for very long, but she was pretty sure that she wouldn't react well to the thought of snakes underfoot or spiders waiting to drop on her.

After they had been forcing their way through the trees for about half an hour, Rikki looked up at Emma, who was striding ahead in the lead.

"Do you have any idea where you're *going*?" Rikki shouted to her.

Emma gritted her teeth, feeling frustrated. She loved Cleo, but her best friend was always so nervous that it meant Emma had never been able to show her fears. She had grown so used to acting confidently and taking charge, she didn't know how to behave any other way. Now this new girl was questioning everything she did, and it felt weird.

"Just *up*," she replied after a pause. She looked all around her at the strange

surroundings. Surely they would reach a clearing soon? Surely there must be *somewhere* on this island that could receive a signal? They just had to keep going and hope that they got a signal before nightfall.

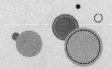

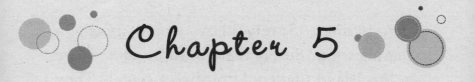

Chapter 5

An hour later, they were still pushing through the thick branches.

"I'm *still* not getting a signal," Emma informed the other girls with a sigh.

"But maybe we won't get a signal," said Cleo, clutching at low-hanging branches to help her keep her balance. "What then? What if we can't call *anyone*? What if *nobody* finds us?"

Cleo's nice, thought Rikki, who really liked her new friend. *But she can be a bit of a whinger.* She knew that Cleo was probably right to be a little worried – but it would help her a lot more to just learn to chill out. Yes, it was scary and dangerous being there without a way off the island, but they would probably find a way home and there was no use worrying about every single thing, most of which wouldn't even happen. Rikki looked at Cleo's back, which was

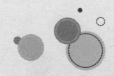

just in front of her, and smiled. It seemed as if Cleo just ran to meet trouble halfway!

"Well, we'll have to draw straws and decide which one of us the others will eat," she said, trying to lighten the atmosphere.

The other two stopped and looked back over their shoulders at her. Cleo's face was tense, but Emma's was just irritated.

"That's not funny!" said Emma.

She knew that her best friend's imagination could totally run away with her, and they didn't need to have to deal with an hysterical Cleo on top of everything else.

"I'm relieving the tension," Rikki replied, holding out her arms in disbelief. Had these girls had some kind of sense-of-humour bypass?

"You're making it worse," moaned Cleo, who was now having visions of cannibals and enormous cooking pots.

"Come *on*!" Emma instructed them, her voice filled with irritation. The sooner she could

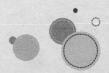

get off this island and away from Rikki Chadwick, the better.

The light began to fade and the shadows cast by the trees and vines of the jungle grew longer all around them. The three girls scrambled further up the side of the island, their arms and legs aching and tired. Emma was getting worried. She really didn't want to have to spend the night in this place. None of them had any warm clothes, and who knew what sort of animals came out at night? Her parents had always warned her to stay away from Mako Island. They said that there were strange rumours about it, and it was a dangerous place. And now here she was, right in the middle of it. *This is all Rikki's fault*, she thought. *Mum and Dad are going to flip out when I get home and they find out where I've been.* She didn't even allow herself to think that she might not *get* home.

Rikki was looking all around her as she climbed, fascinated by this remote island. She

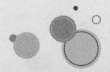

couldn't understand why Emma and Cleo were so scared of it. Sure, it was a bit spooky in the half-light, but that just made it more exciting! *Cleo just needs a bit more confidence*, she decided, *and Emma needs to lighten up once in a while*.

Cleo was concentrating on keeping her balance – Emma was setting a pretty fast pace. She was feeling a little nervous, but having Emma around made her calmer. Emma always knew what to do, and Cleo really appreciated having such a confident, decisive best friend. She glanced back at Rikki, wishing that *she* could understand how great Emma was. But Rikki's expression was unreadable. Cleo tripped over a root and yelped, realizing that she needed to pay more attention to where she was putting her feet.

At long last, they reached a place where the trees opened out into a clearing. In front of them were a number of huge boulders, and Emma hurried forward, scrambling over them.

Cleo followed her unsteadily and Rikki brought up the rear. They scrambled over the rocky surface and then Emma stopped abruptly and looked down. The others came and stood just behind her.

Beneath them, a narrow, fast-flowing creek cascaded down to a larger rock pool. The creek was right in their path – the only way to go any further forward was to jump over it. Looking at the large gap between two boulders, Emma paused.

"Mind your step," she warned the others.

She checked her phone again but there was still no signal. They *had* to get higher. After evaluating the distance between the boulders for a moment, she took a running jump and cleared the gap with ease, using her arms to give her extra momentum and landing as neatly as a gymnast.

Cleo admired Emma's technique – she made it look really easy. But then she leaned forward to look at the drop. The distance between the

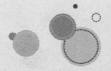

boulders seemed pretty wide. Cleo gulped and shuffled backwards a few steps.

Rikki edged past her and glanced at her for a moment. She could see that Cleo felt nervous, and it *was* a fairly big jump, but if Emma could do it, so could she. With barely a pause, she followed in Emma's steps, making the jump without any problem and landing as smoothly as she had landed in the Zodiac earlier. Then she and Emma looked at Cleo.

Cleo looked up at her friends and then down at the gap she was expected to cross. Her heart was hammering and her legs suddenly felt like cotton wool. She could feel sweat prickling her scalp.

"I can't do this," she said, shaking her head. "It's too slippery. There's *got* to be another way."

Emma shook her head and tried to argue – she had already seen that they had found the best way across the creek. But Cleo wouldn't listen. She looked all around for an easier way

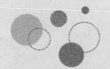

over to Emma and Rikki, and took a tentative step forward. But as her foot touched the slippery boulder, she lost her balance. She screamed, waving her arms to try to stay upright, but it was no use. Cleo slipped and fell, screaming with shock as she tumbled over the ledge and disappeared from sight.

Emma and Rikki watched in horror as Cleo vanished right in front of their eyes.

"*Cleo*!" Emma screamed, looking around desperately for a way to reach her friend.

There was no answer. She and Rikki scrambled back up to the ledge where they'd jumped from and immediately saw where she must have gone. There was a deep, narrow gap in the rock beside the creek, dropping sharply down like a tunnel towards darkness below. They both stood in front of it and peered into the cold blackness, trying to make out what was down there.

"*Cleo*!" Emma called again, beginning to panic. Something, any kind of response from

Cleo would do. Just so they knew she was okay! But they could hear nothing except the rushing of the water over the boulders.

"*Cleo*!" cried Rikki, her voice echoing down the tunnel. Nothing.

"*Cleo*!" both girls yelled as loudly as they could. But the only response they heard was the frightened squawking of a flock of birds.

Cleo had completely disappeared.

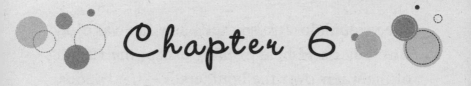

Chapter 6

Cleo was lying on her back at the bottom of the tunnel, fighting for breath. She had hurtled headfirst down the strange gap in the rock at top speed, snagging her clothes on the rough rock and getting bruised and battered all the way. She had finally landed on sandy ground, but the bump had totally winded her. She groaned and tried to sit up. Her ankle twinged and she realized that she must have twisted it on her way down. She rubbed it and looked around, her eyes slowly becoming accustomed to the gloom.

The only faint light was filtering down the tunnel above her. All around her was dark, glistening rock. She was in a small, round cave, deep underground. *This is a nightmare*, she thought. *I knew it was a mistake to come anywhere near this creepy island!* The cave smelled damp and musty, although the sand she

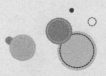

had landed on was dry. Cleo brushed sand off her clothes and gave another little groan as her bruised body ached. Then she heard her friends' voices calling her name.

"*Cleo*!" Emma sounded almost frantic by now.

"I'm okay," Cleo finally managed to gasp out. "I'm fine."

Emma and Rikki heard Cleo's voice drift faintly up out of the hole. Rikki let out a sigh of relief and Emma grinned and felt her body relax. Now that she knew her friend was safe, she was sure that they would find a way to get her out.

"Can you climb up?" she shouted down the tunnel.

"No," said Cleo flatly, shaking her head even though the others couldn't see her. She looked up at the slippery tunnel and realized that there was nothing to grab hold of. There was no way she could get back up there.

"Are you sure?" said Emma, knowing that Cleo sometimes thought things were impossible when they were only difficult. "Come on. Just *try*!"

Emma wanted her friend to instantly reappear safely back on the boulder with them. Cleo rolled her eyes and tried to stand up, but her ankle twinged again and she stopped.

"I can't," she called with defeat in her voice. "There's no way. It's too steep."

Emma knew that Cleo wasn't going to be able to get back up by herself, so there was only one thing for it.

"I've got to go down and get her," she said, turning to Rikki.

Rikki was speechless for a moment. She couldn't believe what she was hearing. Why would anyone deliberately fling themselves down that dark tunnel? There had to be a way out – they just had to convince Cleo to try to climb.

Emma turned back to peer down the tunnel.

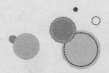

She knew what she had to do, but the dark tunnel looked really, *really* uninviting. Still, Cleo was down there, and she needed help. *There is no way I'm leaving her down there on her own*, she thought. *She'll be petrified.*

"Are you crazy?" Rikki began, finding her voice. "It doesn't make sense if you–"

But Rikki broke off as Emma jumped feet first down the tunnel, letting out a squeal as she disappeared into the dark.

Yep, she's crazy, Rikki thought.

The light that came down the tunnel was blocked out for a moment as Emma shot down it, squealing all the way. Cleo moved to one side as Emma landed with a thud on the sand at the bottom of the tunnel, right beside her.

Emma looked all around in amazement, gazing up at the dark rock that formed the walls of the little cave. This was a very, very weird place. It was so perfectly shaped that it was

almost as if someone had created it – as if it wasn't a natural cave at all. But who would bother to come all the way out to a remote island and carve out a cave where no one would ever see it?

Cleo just stared at her, wondering what they were going to do next, but very glad that her best friend was now beside her. Finally Emma looked at Cleo and snapped out of her reverie.

"Are you okay?" she asked.

"My leg hurts a little," Cleo answered quietly.

Emma glanced at it and saw that there was nothing obviously wrong. She rubbed it and smiled at Cleo.

"It's probably just sprained," she said in her most reassuring voice. "We can–"

But she broke off as a slithering, bumping noise grew louder. They heard Rikki yelling, and then she shot out of the tunnel like a rocket and crashed into Emma and Cleo.

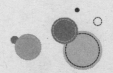

"Whoah!" Rikki shouted. She gazed around the little cave, just as the others had done.

"*What* are you doing here?" Emma asked her, feeling totally exasperated. Was everything going to go wrong today?

"Well *you* came down!" Rikki answered, immediately on the defensive. She wasn't going to be left out of the rescue attempt.

"You were meant to stay up the top and throw down a rope or something," Emma said straight away, pointing back up the tunnel.

"What am I – a mind reader?" Rikki exclaimed, throwing out her arms in disbelief. "And what rope?" she added.

This is hardly the time for arguments, thought Cleo, *and my foot hurts!*

"Shouldn't we concentrate on getting out of here?" she asked, hoping that her friends would stop arguing long enough to listen to a sensible suggestion.

There was a pause as Rikki and Emma

glared at each other. Then they seemed to agree that Cleo was right.

"Yep," they replied in unison.

The three girls got to their feet and started looking around the cave. Cleo's ankle soon stopped aching as she concentrated on looking for an escape route. It wasn't easy to search in the gloom of the cave, and it looked as if the tunnel was the only way in or out. Cleo started to imagine what they would do if they were stuck down there. How would anyone find them in time? No one knew where they were, and they had only found the tunnel by chance – it was completely hidden from view. *We're in big trouble*, thought Cleo.

Outside, the afternoon was drawing to a close and the tide was coming in. Their little boat was not far enough up the beach to stay out of the reach of the waves. But the girls had more important things to worry about than what was happening to Zane's Zodiac. They were working

their way around the cave, searching for something – *anything* – that would help them to escape.

"There's no way out," said Cleo. *We'll be stuck down here forever and no one will ever find us!* she added in her thoughts.

"Let's try here," said Emma, who was examining the far end of the cave. It was the only place they hadn't searched, and it looked like a dead end. Cleo followed Emma across the cave, but she wasn't holding out much hope. She was just imagining how their skeletons would be found huddled together, when Emma gave a cry of triumph.

What had looked like a dead end was actually a narrow gap in the rock. Emma stepped up and peered through the gap. She beckoned for the others to follow her and led the way in.

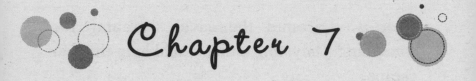

Chapter 7

Strangely, although it was dark, there was a faint light coming from up ahead. *And that means there's got to be another way out*, thought Emma with relief. She knew that night was falling, and that would make it even harder to escape. It was a race against time now.

Emma scrambled up the rocky incline, speaking encouraging words to Cleo, her voice echoing in the enclosed space. Again, it seemed almost as if someone had worked on the rock. Little ridges had been cut into the boulders, which made climbing a lot easier. Cleo was close behind her. Rikki was feeling kind of excited. *This is a real adventure!* she told herself. *And at least we're heading in the right direction – up!*

After a few minutes of steep climbing, the narrow path opened up and led them out into another cave. In spite of her hurry, Emma

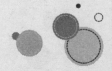

stopped and gasped. Behind her, Cleo stared in wonder. Rikki, who was at the back, peered over their shoulders and gazed around in astonishment. A smile lit up her face.

The cave they found themselves in was spectacular. They were standing on a narrow ledge that opened out around the edge of the cave. There was sand underfoot here too. The rest of the cave floor was a stunning rock pool, filled with azure-blue water that seemed to be lit from below by a soft, glowing light. In fact, the light was so strong that it even flickered around the walls of the cave, faintly pulsating almost as if it were alive.

The girls looked up. The roof of the cave was very high, rising in a cone shape to a round opening at the very top. Through it, they could see the dark, velvety blue of the night sky, dotted with stars. Starlight was shining down through the opening, sparkling on the surface of the pool, filling the cave with glittering light.

Emma, Cleo and Rikki gazed and gazed,

staggered by the sight that met their eyes. It was the most beautiful place any of them had ever seen. It was the kind of place to be kept secret; it just had that kind of vibe – somewhere to be kept secret between friends. It was like somewhere from another world or another time.

"Wow," said Rikki, who was never lost for words for long. "This is like the cone of ... a volcano."

She turned in a full circle and stared up through the opening in the roof of the cave.

"It's, um, not going to erupt, is it?" asked Cleo nervously.

Emma had been feeling almost hypnotized by the shimmering lights. Cleo's words jogged her out of her trance and she turned to her friend with a smile.

"It's been dormant for 20,000 years – I think we're safe," she answered.

They moved further in to the cave, and Emma looked down at edge of the gleaming

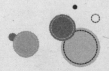

pool. Then she crouched down beside it. Something had caught her eye.

"Look, tidal rings," she said, pointing. "The level of the pool rises and falls."

Her voice was animated and excited.

"*So*?" asked Rikki, getting irritated again. It was kind of annoying how Emma *always* seemed to know something she didn't.

"*So*," explained Emma, swiftly pulling off her shoes, "it's connected to the ocean. There might be a way out."

She stood up, glanced at Rikki and Cleo, and then stepped forward. Without another word, she plunged into the clear water and disappeared from sight.

Rikki and Cleo dropped to their knees, peering into the depths of the pool and trying to see Emma. Cleo wasn't exactly surprised – Emma had always been the one to take charge in any situation. But Rikki was amazed. She found herself feeling a new respect for Emma. It

couldn't have been easy to just dive into the cold water like that, not knowing what she was going to find. She knew that Emma was a strong swimmer, but this was really brave.

Cleo was feeling more anxious than admiring. Now that Emma had gone, she suddenly felt very alone. Rikki was so unpredictable, and they were stuck in yet another cave … albeit a very beautiful one.

"I'm not going to like this," she said, shaking her head and hunching up her shoulders.

For what seemed like ages, Rikki and Cleo watched the pool's surface, waiting for Emma to reappear. Cleo sat cross-legged, getting more and more tense as the minutes ticked by. She felt glad that she could see the sky. It didn't feel so much like they were trapped horribly underground – even though they were. She tapped her hand against her leg and joggled her knee up and down. Somehow it made her feel better.

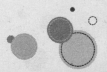

Rikki had taken a more relaxed pose, resting her arms casually on her knees. But she kept glancing down at her watch. *If she's not back in another two minutes, I'm gonna go after her*, she told herself. She remembered what Cleo had said about sharks, and then decided it was best not to think about that.

The silence became too much to bear for Cleo.

"Emma! Emma!" she shouted out into the empty cave. But she heard nothing except her own echoing voice in reply. Rikki's nerves jangled.

"Relax," Rikki said, rolling her eyes. "Just give her a minute."

Suddenly a shimmering, familiar outline appeared below the surface, followed quickly by Emma's confident face looking up at them. Cleo was reminded of the training session at the pool that morning ... had it really only been that morning? It seemed like a lifetime ago.

Emma drew in a deep breath and smiled.

"I was right!" she said. "It's about a 20-second swim to the reef outside – straight through, plenty of room. We can all fit."

There wasn't a trace of doubt in her voice. Rikki was impressed and started to pull off her shoes, but Cleo could hardly believe what she was hearing. *Emma can't seriously expect me to do this*, she thought. *She must have gone completely mad.*

"Through there?" she said, pointing down into the rock pool. "No way."

She clenched her fist and started tapping it against her leg.

Emma recognized Cleo's look of stubborn fear. *Oh no*, she thought. *It's gonna take forever to persuade her, and we don't have the time for this!* She was trying to think of the words that would make Cleo get into the water, but before she could say anything, Rikki had turned an incredulous face on Cleo.

"Go on, Cleo," she said. "There's no other way out. You can do it."

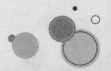

"I *can't* do it," Cleo said, frustrated. "And besides ... I ... I can't swim."

She was embarrassed to admit it in front of Rikki, but they had to understand how impossible it was for her to do what they were asking. There was no way that she could swim underwater even for two seconds, let alone 20. They would have to go without her!

Outside, the full moon was moving slowly across the sky, lighting up the dark ocean and illuminating the highest peaks of Mako Island. It was almost directly over the cave where the girls were trapped. A strange mist was wreathing around the top of the volcano, and the moon seemed to be glowing extra bright, with a pearly blue glow all around it. There were no electric lights for miles around – no sign of civilization. The ink-black waves lapped the shores of Mako Island. It seemed as if everything was waiting – waiting for just the right moment. It was almost time.

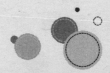

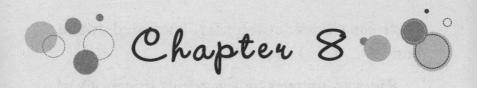

Chapter 8

Finally, Rikki persuaded Cleo to take off her shoes and socks. Each of the three girls tied her shoes around her neck. Then Rikki slipped into the water beside Emma, gasping a little at the chill of it. It felt very odd to be in the water with all her clothes on. She smiled at Emma as she trod water.

Now it was Cleo's turn. She sat on the edge and dipped her feet into the water. Rikki and Emma beckoned her on, but Cleo seemed to have frozen. She stayed on the side, hugging her knees and unable to move any further.

"Everything will be *fine*," Emma said, smiling confidently up at her best friend.

"How can you be sure?" Cleo asked. *Emma doesn't know what it's like!* she thought. *She's been swimming since she was tiny!* Cleo could think of 20 different things that could go wrong

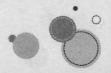

while she was underwater, and they all petrified her.

Rikki swam over to the side of the pool and looked up at Cleo.

"*Listen* to her, Cleo," insisted Rikki. "What alternative do we have? Stay stuck down here forever?"

Cleo glanced around, half contemplating the idea. She thought about her family and her little sister. What if she never saw them again? That decided it – she had to do this, however hard it was. She gave a tiny shrug.

Understanding that the moment had come, Rikki held her hand out. After a long moment, Cleo took it and slid gingerly into the water. Then she just kept on sinking, disappearing below the surface. Without hesitation, Rikki dived down and pulled her back up again. Emma held her gaze steadily as she moved towards her.

Cleo held on tightly to Rikki's hand and Emma took her other hand. Then Emma and

Rikki held hands to steady themselves, so they formed a circle. In a low, reassuring voice, Emma told Cleo how to tread water. They stayed in that position, right underneath the hole at the top of the cave, as Cleo got used to the sensation of being in the water. It was really buoyant, which helped, but Cleo was still way, *way* out of her comfort zone.

Rikki and Emma were concentrating hard on helping Cleo, and Cleo was concentrating hard on staying afloat and not panicking, so no one noticed that the full moon had now moved directly over the cave. It was framed by the perfect hole in the cave roof.

Then a shaft of moonlight from above shone down onto the pool, just where the girls were treading water, and the cave was suddenly filled with a brilliant light. Without warning, the water around them began to foam and bubble.

The girls clung to each other, unable to speak or move. They were lit up in a column of

moonlight, and the white, foamy water gathered around them. Then bright bubbles were lifted from the water's surface, each one glowing in the light of the moon. The bubbles whirled around their heads and rose upwards, as if the moon was somehow controlling them. Up, up, up, until they reached the hole at the top of the cone-shaped cave.

The moon was so bright that the girls couldn't see what happened to the bubbles – they just seemed to turn into a glowing, silvery-blue mist high above. It felt as if they were in the middle of the Milky Way – the bubbles of water were shining as bright as stars, and all they could see was light. It was as if the walls of the cave had completely vanished. There was just the light, the water and the three girls.

After a few moments, the light seemed to become less intense and to fade. The last bubbles rose and the water around them stopped frothing so much.

"*Wow*," said Cleo.

She had totally forgotten her fears of being in the water.

"Spooky," said Emma, frowning a little.

Rikki said nothing. She was still watching the water around them as it stopped bubbling and foaming. *I've never seen anything like that before,* she thought. *What was that?*

Something *very* strange had just happened; all three girls had felt it. They held on to each other, finding the close presence of the others comforting. Without needing to say a word, they knew that they would have to talk about what had just happened and try to understand it. But right now, there was no time to talk about anything. Right now, they had to focus on getting out of that cave.

"Okay, now concentrate," said Emma, speaking to Cleo. "Take a deep breath."

Cleo nodded and turned to her friends. She was suddenly finding it surprisingly easy to tread water, and for some reason the water didn't feel quite as alien to her as it had before.

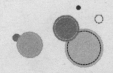

Emma looked at them both, smiled encouragingly and then inhaled a huge breath and swam down. She dived through the hole at the back of the cave and on along the narrow, rocky tunnel that she had discovered earlier.

Emma swam confidently through the strange underwater caverns, past barnacle-encrusted rocks, huge, other-worldly plants and finger-like fronds that seemed to reach out to touch her. It was further than she had said, but she knew that the others could do it and she hadn't wanted to scare Cleo. She thrust herself forward with her strong legs, and soon she emerged from the caves and swam swiftly upwards to the surface.

Back in the volcano cave, Rikki looked at Cleo and gave a little nod, half questioning and half encouraging. Cleo nodded back. On the count of three, they filled their lungs as full as they could, and then followed Emma down.

Cleo and Rikki swam close beside each other, holding hands. Rikki showed Cleo how to move

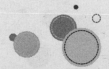

her other arm and how to kick her legs. Cleo found that she had no difficulty swimming, although it had always seemed impossible when she had tried it before. They swam steadily through the hole at the back of the cave and along the narrow tunnel. Cleo tried to control her feelings of panic as the fronds and plants brushed against her, but her hand gripped Rikki's so hard that Rikki grimaced in pain. At last they swam out of the tunnel and kicked their way gratefully up to the surface, their lungs bursting with the need for air.

Rikki and Cleo surfaced next to Emma, in the open sea. They were all coughing and spluttering. Cleo gasped for breath.

"That was more than 20 seconds!" she exclaimed as soon as she could speak.

"Oh relax, we made it didn't we?" Rikki said. *Really! It's whine, whine, whine with Cleo sometimes*, she thought.

"I'm proud of you, Cleo," said Emma. "I knew you could do it."

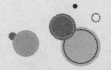

Before Emma had time to think about what to do next, or Cleo had time to panic about sharks, a strong beam of light shone in their faces and a loud siren almost deafened them. They held up their hands to protect their eyes, and heard a voice booming at them through a megaphone.

"This is the Water Police," the voice yelled. "Please make your way to the boarding ladder at the rear of the vessel."

In front of them, a white rescue boat was bobbing up and down, and a searchlight was scanning the water.

"Come on," said Emma, striking out towards the boat. Rikki was right beside her, matching her stroke for stroke. They were saved!

But Cleo paused for a moment, treading water, and looked back over her shoulder. The moon was still directly above Mako Island, and the tall rocks were bathed in a cold, bluish light. Strands of cloud were wrapped around the highest peaks. It looked very eerie.

Cleo gave it a final, suspicious glance, and then followed her friends. She had never thought she would be so grateful to see a boat.

Cleo climbed up the boarding ladder, shivering with cold and fear. Emma and Cleo were already on board, wrapped in blankets, and someone put a warm blanket around Cleo's shoulders. The three girls sat huddled together, sipping hot tea from a flask and listening to the Water Police officers explain what had happened.

Their parents had called the police when they hadn't come home, and someone had reported seeing three girls heading out to sea in a little boat. The Water Police had sent all their vessels straight out and had been sweeping the water when they saw the girls' heads bob up.

As they sped to shore, Cleo explained how Zane had stranded her in the Zodiac and Rikki had rescued her. The officers gave them a lecture about heading too far out to sea and

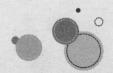

about 'borrowing' spark plugs, but the girls could tell that they were just happy to have found them. The officers also said that there was no excuse at all for what Zane had done, and that they would be paying a little visit to his dad. The girls exchanged glances and grinned.

Their parents were waiting for them on the shore with warm clothes and more lectures. Finally the girls were whisked home to bed and sleep. It had been a very long, very weird day.

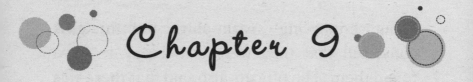

Chapter 9

The next morning looked like it was going to be the start of another beautiful day. The sun rose in a clear, cloud-free sky, warming the sand and the sea. Emma woke early, despite her adventures of the day before, and jumped out of bed. She always went down to the beach for an early-morning swim, but today she felt especially drawn to the sea. As much as she loved training and doing laps at the pool, swimming at the beach was where she felt truly free. It was just her and the waves – no clocks, no lanes, no restrictions. She couldn't remember a time when she hadn't felt completely at home in the water.

She stopped a little way up the beach, dropped her bag and unwrapped her towel. She was wearing her favourite blue bikini. She gazed out to the horizon, and then watched the waves

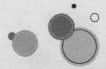

breaking into white foam as they approached the shore.

Emma frowned – the foam reminded her of that strange moment in the cave the night before. She decided that after her swim she would go over to Cleo's and talk it all through. But right now, it was time to enjoy herself.

She raced down to the water's edge and plunged into the water with a shallow dive. She grinned, relishing the sensation of the cool water sliding around her body as her strong limbs sliced through the waves. Then she surfaced, feeling the morning sun shining down on her face and revelling in the cool water that lapped around her.

But as she paused, treading water, she began to feel a bizarre sensation from her hips down to her toes, like pins and needles! It wasn't numbness exactly, more like ... well she didn't know what! It wasn't exactly like cramp, and she hadn't been bitten. But she couldn't seem to feel her toes. Emma had never known anything like

it. She began to lurch about unsteadily, just like Cleo had the night before when she had been learning how to tread water.

This is ridiculous, she thought. *I know how to swim; I've been doing it for long enough!* But it felt as though she couldn't kick her legs. Emma peered into the water to see if there was some kelp or a net or something that had wrapped itself around her legs. She squinted down into the water, expecting to see something horrible wrapped around her legs. But instead she saw something she'd definitely never expected to see in a million years. Where her legs had been, she had ... she had ... a *tail*!

Emma gave a high-pitched squeak of fear and looked around. This had to be a trick, right? There was no one else in the water – no one to help her or to blame. But deep inside, Emma knew that it was no trick. The tail felt like part of her – she knew exactly how to move it and she could feel the water on it, just as she usually could with her legs. Her blue bikini had

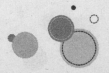

completely vanished, and the top half had been replaced with what looked like … scales! Emma slowly moved the tail and held herself in position, hoping that she would wake up. This was just too weird!

At the same time, not far from the beach, Cleo was lying in the bath. Her younger sister, Kim, was banging on the door.

"Come on Cleo, you can't stay in there forever!" she yelled.

Cleo stared in disbelief at her tail. *Wanna bet?* she thought.

"*Cleo*!" Kim hollered. Her sister had been in the bathroom for an hour already, and she didn't think she could hold on for much longer.

Cleo barely heard her as she gazed unblinkingly at the scaly, pale-gold tail that was hanging over the edge of the bath and dripping water onto the floor. Cleo flapped the tail weakly.

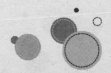

She had woken up early, longing for a bath. The night before she had been too tired to do anything except fall into bed, but now she felt surprisingly energetic. She had run the water, poured in half a bottle of bubble bath and locked the door. Then she had stepped into the bath, sat down and leaned back, ready for a bit of pampering.

But her enjoyment hadn't lasted long. Suddenly she had started to feel a very peculiar sensation up and down her legs. Next minute … *this*! Cleo reached out and very, *very* gingerly patted the tail. It felt just like touching her own skin. She pinched it and winced as she felt the pain. The bath water was almost cold but she hardly noticed.

"*Cleo!*" yelled Kim again.

But Cleo wasn't moving. *This has to be a dream*, she told herself. *Or some kind of hallucination. Maybe I swallowed too much sea water last night! Yeah, that's it, too much sea water … always makes you hallucinate that*

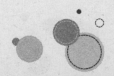

you've turned into a super-size fish!

But somehow she knew that this was all too real. She wasn't hallucinating the bits of bubble bath that still clung to the tail, or her sister's whining voice outside the door.

She thought about calling for her parents, but then she heard her father leaving for work and her mother calling Kim to go shopping. Kim left, shouting a few final insults through the door as she went. Besides, what would she say to them? Cleo didn't think she could bear anyone else's reaction right now – she was having a hard enough time dealing with her own reaction.

Cleo pulled the plug out of the bath and felt the water drain away. Her expression didn't change, but her imagination was running riot. How was she supposed to go to school like this? How was she supposed to get a job or go to the café or sit exams or go shopping? How was she even supposed to get out of the bath?

The bathroom window was open and a warm breeze was blowing in, flowing over her skin

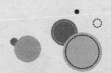

(and her scales!) and drying them. It felt kind of nice. Cleo took a deep breath and tried to imagine what Emma would say if she were here. Her advice would be to keep calm, to think this through. Then Cleo jumped and her tail gave another little wiggle. That's it! she said to herself. I'll ask Emma! She'll know what to do for the best.

Now that she had a plan, Cleo felt better already. She just had to figure out a way to get to the phone …

Not far away, Rikki was wandering through the park beside the marina, wondering if it was too early to go and call on Cleo. She had woken up early that morning after a night full of dreams, packed with mysterious lights and underwater caves. She had leapt out of bed and decided that she really wanted to go for a walk beside the water. She somehow felt as though it would make her thoughts clearer.

Rikki really wanted to discuss with the others what had happened the night before – especially

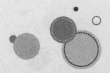

that strange moment in the cave. Her quick mind had already formed a hazy plan. If she could just persuade Emma and Cleo to go back to Mako Island with her, she was sure that they could find out more. After all, it wasn't dangerous – not now they knew the secret escape route from the cave. They could moor a boat out at sea and just swim straight in to the cave. *I'm sure Emma would be up for it*, she thought. *Admittedly, she might take a bit more persuading!*

She looked over at the boats in the marina and grinned, thinking about the night before. The Water Police had been awesome. Zane's Zodiac was probably still on the beach at Mako Island – if the tide hadn't swept it away. Rikki laughed to herself. *Serves him right!* she thought.

As she passed the marina, Rikki heard the *ch-ch-ch* sound of an automated sprinkler system starting up. They were dotted about all over the park and as it was going to be a hot day, this was the best way to keep the grass and the

plants green.

Rikki glanced around to see where the sprinkler was, but it was camouflaged and she couldn't see it. Then the cool drops from the sprinkler flew towards her, raining down on her and gently covering her from head to toe. Within a couple of seconds she was soaked to the skin.

Irritated, Rikki raised up her arms and shook the water off them, looking down to see how badly her clothes had been affected. Then she began to feel the strangest sensation in her legs ... and not just her legs, but all over her body. Tiny, bright bubbles of water, just like the ones they had seen last night, seemed to be clinging all over her body. She looked down and drew in her breath in fear and amazement – for a moment it was as if her entire body was made of nothing but *water*! Then she felt herself falling. She tried to move her legs, but they wouldn't respond.

"What's happ–" she said as she fell forward,

face first, onto the grass.

The automated sprinkler stopped spraying water and Rikki tried to raise herself up, but she could only lift her upper body off the ground. She still couldn't move her legs. Full of trepidation, Rikki turned her head and looked over her shoulder. Her mouth fell open as she stared at the long, scale-covered tail where her legs should have been.

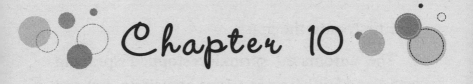

Chapter 10

Three panicked phone calls later, Emma and Rikki were heading over to Cleo's house as fast as they could; they desperately needed to talk! Cleo's house was beautiful. It was right on the water and was surrounded by tall palm trees. But Rikki barely noticed it as she dashed up to the house – she couldn't wait to talk to the others about what had happened. Emma ran up behind her as she knocked and all three of them began talking as soon as Cleo opened the front door.

"It was orange and *covered* with scales," Cleo told her friends, her eyes still wide with alarm.

Emma strode through the house to the sitting room, followed closely by the others. "The minute I hit water–" Emma said, barely listening to Cleo.

She was interrupted by Rikki, who could

78

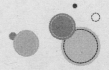

hardly contain herself.

"I *was* water for a second," she said, gesticulating wildly, remembering how she had been completely transparent.

Emma sat down in an armchair and Cleo turned to Rikki.

"I was a *fish*!" she said, half hoping that one of the others would have a rational explanation.

"Hey, what's going on?" said Rikki, who was hoping the same thing.

"That's what *I* want to know!" Emma said over the top of them both.

All three of them paused for a moment. Cleo flopped down onto the sofa. It was scary just saying what had happened out loud, but at least it sounded as if they had all had the same experience. She wouldn't want anyone else to hear them though ...

Rikki and Emma looked at each other. They had both just had exactly the same thought.

"Is there anyone else here?" Rikki asked,

suddenly feeling the need for caution.

"No, Dad's at work and my sister and Mum are shopping," Cleo told them, tucking her feet underneath her.

Reassured that they were alone, Rikki perched on the arm of Emma's chair. She was feeling really shaky and a little out of her depth. Just what was going on here?

Emma took a deep breath. She needed to take control of the situation somehow. *We have to be able to work this out,* she thought. *Let's start at the beginning.*

"Okay, what happened to us?" she began.

Cleo shrugged, unable to even begin to answer, but Rikki had caught on to what Emma was trying to do. They had to go over the events step by step.

"About ten seconds after we touch water, we ..." Rikki's words failed her when she tried to describe what she had just seen, "... we grow these ..."

"And it vanishes when we're dry," Cleo continued hastily, not sure if she was ready to hear the word 'tail'. "And that's the same with you two – right?"

She raised her eyebrows questioningly and looked at Emma.

"Yeah," Emma agreed, looking very serious.

Rikki nodded too, her expression alternating between a smile and a frown. This was scary and cool at the same time!

Cleo continued slowly, her eyes fixed on her best friend. "The ... *tails* ... are like ..."

She stopped, unable to express the thought that was in her head. It sounded crazy even *before* it had been spoken – she couldn't say it out loud.

"Exactly like ..." said Emma, and then she stopped as well, looking down at the floor. Her forehead crinkled in a frown and she waved her hand in the air vaguely. She felt embarrassed just *thinking* it.

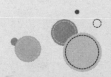

But the fear of sounding crazy had never stopped Rikki before.

"We look like … *mermaids*," she said, smiling a little. Memories of magical stories from childhood fairy tales were floating through her mind.

Emma whipped her head around so fast that her long blonde ponytail slapped Rikki's arm.

"I've told you before, you're *not* funny," she snapped. "Mermaids *don't* exist." She paused, and then her voice softened. Deep inside, she knew that Rikki was only saying what they were all thinking. "That's just … too weird," she added more gently.

She turned her head aside again and for a moment no one said anything.

The three girls stared into space, trying to think of what to do or say next. Each of them felt as if she had just been punched, or hit around the head, or something. This simply didn't make sense.

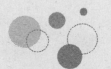

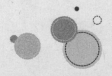

Emma was not enjoying this feeling of helplessness – she wasn't used to it. They couldn't just ask their parents – if they sounded crazy to each other, imagine what their parents would think! That applied to teachers as well, and it wasn't as if there were any books or internet sites available on 'what to do if you get turned into a mermaid'.

Cleo was still in shock, and just one thought kept repeating itself in her head like a broken record. *I am a fish ... I am a fish ...*

Rikki's mind was whirling and sparking like a Catherine wheel. She didn't seem able to hold on to a single clear thought. Could they even *drink* water without growing tails? Would this last forever? Would they get their legs back if it happened again? Was this horrific or exciting?

Then there was a knock on the front door.

All three girls jumped out of their skins. They stared at each other, bound together by a common secret. What if someone had overheard something through an open window?

Cleo tensed in fear, and then relaxed as she realized who it must be at the door.

"Oh *no*," she said, closing her eyes and shaking her head. "It's Lewis. I forgot, he's helping me with biology today."

Cleo had been friends with Lewis McCartney since they were five years old. He was kind of a nerd, but he was also very kind and incredibly loyal. Cleo really liked him, but right now he was the last person she wanted to see. Lewis could usually guess that something was wrong just by looking at her! She jumped up and dashed towards the hallway as she heard Lewis letting himself in.

Chapter 11

"Cleo!" Lewis called.

Cleo rushed out into the hallway just as Lewis was shutting the door.

"Cle ... oh!" he said as he turned and saw her behind him. He noted her guilty expression and then saw Emma and Rikki behind her, looking up at him. Rikki remained expressionless, and Emma gave him a tight little smile.

Lewis looked suddenly awkward and nervous, which was how he always felt around girls – especially cool, confident girls like Rikki and Emma. It was different with Cleo – she always put him at his ease.

"Oh," he said again, walking into the sitting room with his biology books under his arm. "Er ... did I get the time wrong?"

He glanced down at his watch as he walked

85

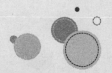

past Emma and Rikki towards the dining table where he and Cleo always studied. Emma and Rikki just watched him as he walked, which made him feel even more self conscious.

"No, we said nine," said Cleo, following him over to the table and trying to keep her voice relaxed. "But ... sorry, Lewis ... something *has* come up."

"Like what?" Lewis asked, dropping his books onto the table.

Cleo looked at Emma and Rikki, who were as still as statues.

"Just something important ..." said Cleo slowly, racking her brain for a suitable excuse. *What do I say? What do I say?* She glanced at Rikki and Emma again. They both looked seriously alarmed. Emma flashed her a warning look and Rikki shook her head. Lewis saw that and his confusion grew deeper. "... but ... not *so* important that you need to know about it," Cleo finished, knowing how lame she sounded. "Sorry, Lewis. I have to cancel."

She put a hand on his back and guided him back in the direction of the front door. Lewis frowned, and then looked disappointed.

"Oh," he said as he walked back past Rikki and Emma, darting nervous glances at them. "Um, maybe some other time?"

He paused in the hallway, looking at Emma and Rikki as if they were some rare and dangerous type of plant life.

Emma and Rikki relaxed – he was going. *Stay calm, stay calm*, thought Rikki. But then Cleo had a brainwave. She glanced at the other girls and then made her mind up.

"Lewis, you're smart," she stated. "Do you know anything about mermaids?"

Cleo had acted on impulse, and the other girls didn't have a chance to stop her before the words were out. Rikki rolled her eyes and stared up at the ceiling. Was Cleo crazy? Was she actually going to *tell* this nerdy boy what had happened to them? Her hands moved involuntarily to her head and she dropped them

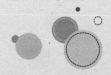

quickly, realizing that clutching her hair was not a calm look.

Emma just closed her eyes, feeling a sort of deadly despair sweep over her. *Please tell me she didn't just say that*, she thought. *Loony bin here we come.* She opened her eyes and looked over at Lewis, who was staring at Cleo as if he thought she was mad – which Emma could completely understand.

"No, not really," he said after a long pause. Lewis always hated admitting ignorance on any subject.

"Okay," said Cleo, herding him towards the door. "Sorry. Bye."

She virtually pushed him out of the door. He looked at her as if he was going to say something else, but she didn't give him the chance. She closed the door behind him and turned to find both Rikki and Emma on their feet, shoulder to shoulder. They were both looking very annoyed. In fact, they had never looked so much in agreement.

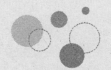

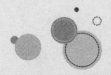

"What?" Cleo asked with a little shrug, although she knew perfectly well what was coming.

Emma was speechless. She looked at Rikki, who opened her eyes wide and put on a high-pitched, dopey-sounding voice.

"Do you know anything about mermaids?" she said, imitating Cleo before reverting to her usual tone to add, "Are you *crazy*?"

"Cleo, this is really serious," said Emma, trying to make her friend understand how worried she was. "If anyone found out about this, we could be in *big* trouble."

"Well, maybe ..." Cleo began, not entirely sure where she was going with her excuses. There was a part of her that thought they should just call up their parents and tell them everything. Parents always knew what to do, right?

"Look, something very strange has happened to us," Emma said. "We don't know how, and we

certainly don't know why."

With Emma's words, all three girls again felt a sense of being bound together, them against the world. Rikki looked at Emma. *She's actually making sense for once*, she thought. *But there's only one thing we can do right now.* A small smile flickered over her expressive face.

"There is a way for us to find out more," she said, looking from Emma to Cleo.

"How?" Cleo asked, frowning at her.

"Go back in the water!" said Rikki, as if it was the most obvious thing in the world.

"No way," said Cleo firmly, shaking her head. "Not me."

She flashed a disbelieving smile at Emma, fully expecting her best friend to back her up. But Emma was nodding at Rikki. Cleo strode over to the armchair, sat down and folded her arms. Emma and Rikki followed and sat beside her, one on each arm of the chair.

"*I'm* going," Rikki continued, speaking

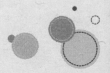

slowly and meaningfully. "I just … don't think I should go *alone*. Any volunteers?"

She exchanged a nod with Emma and looked down at Cleo, who looked gravely back up at her. She could feel Emma's hand resting gently on her shoulder and she knew that they were both about to try to persuade her to do what they said. *But not this time*, Cleo thought. *We're not trapped in an underwater cave now – I've got a choice. There is no way I am going to deliberately jump into the water and turn into a fish, just so Rikki can get her kicks.*

Rikki started to try to talk Cleo round. Her powers of persuasion were excellent and she was sure that it wouldn't take long to get Cleo on side. But Emma sighed. She knew the expression on Cleo's face all too well. When she had made a firm decision about something, there was no one more stubborn. Some people at school thought that Cleo was a bit of a pushover because she was so gentle, but Emma knew better, and Rikki was about to find out the truth – the hard way.

Rikki spent a solid hour trying to persuade Cleo to come with them. But it was no use – Cleo just kept shaking her head with her arms folded tightly across her chest. It was like trying to argue with a big stone wall. Emma joined in as well, trying everything to make Cleo change her mind. She really wanted it to be the three of them – it felt as if that was important. But time was marching on and finally they had to give up.

Emma and Rikki left Cleo at her house and headed off to get their swimming gear. Then they walked down to a remote part of the beach in silence. They didn't want anyone to see what happened to them when they walked into the water. But whatever was going on here, they were both determined to find some answers.

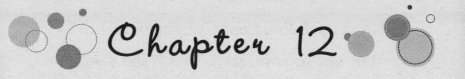

Chapter 12

Rikki and Emma walked down to the beach on the rocks, being very careful not to tread in any water on the way. They were both dressed in knee-length shorts and bikini tops. Their hair was carefully tied back.

They stood on the furthest rock and looked out over the blue, foam-flecked ocean. Rikki put her hands on her hips, wondering what would happen when they went into the water. What if *nothing* happened? Was it going to be just some kind of strange, one-off shared delusion that they could put down to a late night and a police rescue? Or was it something more *sinister*? She couldn't wait to find out!

Emma folded her arms and looked at Rikki. Now that the moment had come, she found herself hesitating. It felt very weird to be nervous about getting into the water. *This must*

 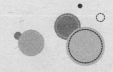

be how Cleo feels all the time, she thought.

"I'm not so sure about this," she said, half turning to Rikki.

"It's all right. I am," said Rikki, happily.

"That gives me *no* confidence whatsoever," Emma replied, but she couldn't help giving a smile. As she got to know Rikki better, she was liking her more and more. She loved Cleo, but it was a new and exciting experience to have a friend who pushed her into trying new things for once.

Rikki smiled back, understanding that Emma was half teasing her. She jumped down off the rock and stood a couple of feet from the water's edge. Emma followed her and they walked forward together, instinctively reaching for each other's hand.

"About ten seconds, right?" Rikki asked as soon as their feet hit the water.

"Yep," Emma replied with a little frown of concentration.

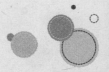

They started to count aloud together.

"One, two, three, four ..."

They hadn't even reached five before they felt a tingling sensation in their legs. Their hair was suddenly floating free – their hair bands had disappeared. So had their legs. They toppled face first into the water, their tails flapping behind them in the sand.

Lying on their stomachs, the girls raised their upper bodies out of the water, flicking the water out of their faces. Emma looked over at Rikki and couldn't repress a wide smile. This was weird and unnerving – but it felt really exciting! Rikki laughed too, and then shrugged in half disbelief. It had been strange enough to see herself with a tail – to see Emma with a tail was just bizarre. *So we're fish, just like Cleo said*, she thought. *I guess it wasn't just a delusion, then!*

They flapped their tails in the shallows experimentally, and then agreed that there was only one thing for it. They would have to try out

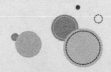

their new bodies in deep water. It was time to go diving.

They struck out to sea and then plunged down to the ocean floor.

The first thing that Emma noticed was how long she could stay underwater without needing to come up for air. She didn't even seem to need to hold her breath. It was amazing. Also she was easily able to keep her eyes open without them stinging or feeling sore, whereas usually she always wore goggles to swim underwater.

At first the girls stayed close to shore, practising using their tails. Emma found that she didn't need to use her arms in the same way as before. Instead she stretched her arms out in front of her, turning her body into one, long shape that moved like a wave, undulating up and down. She experimented with swimming upside down while Rikki twisted and turned through the water.

They played hide and seek among huge, sea-sculpted boulders. They swam with fish and

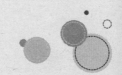

raced each other from place to place. They stayed close together, curving around each other and exploring the underwater rocks and plants. Then they grew more daring and separated a little more, darting between brightly coloured corals and zooming through natural underwater archways.

The two girls grew gradually more adventurous. Rikki found that by giving rapid, tiny flicks of her tail, she could spin through the water as she swam, rotating like some kind of drill. *This is like the biggest fairground ride of all time!* she thought as she zoomed past Emma, grinning and waving. Emma was just enjoying the freedom to move however she wanted in the water with complete control. She couldn't stop smiling. She couldn't remember the last time she had had so much fun!

They met a young dolphin and followed it further out to sea, encouraged by its welcoming clicking sounds. It showed them places they had never known existed and played tag with them in the dark-blue depths. It took them to see an

old wrecked boat that was half buried in the sand at the bottom of the ocean, just like it was showing them a secret den. Both girls felt as if they had made a new friend.

Although they were out further and deeper than they had ever swum before, they didn't feel cold. The water just seemed pleasantly warm, and it felt as natural to be there as it did to be on land. Even Emma, who had always thought she felt totally at ease in the water, realized that she hadn't been completely at home in it. It was as if they were a part of the ocean, and the ocean was really glad to have them.

The sun filtered through the water, lighting up their strange new world, and they were both filled with an overwhelming sense of joy. They smiled at each other, sharing the same feeling of bubbling, ecstatic excitement. This wasn't something to be *afraid* of. This was a *gift*!

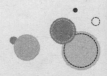

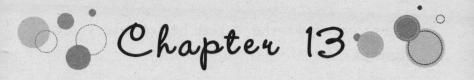

Chapter 13

Meanwhile, Cleo was sitting at home, feeling hurt and upset. She hated it when anyone tried to persuade her to do something that she couldn't, and Rikki had really tried everything to get her to change her mind. But Cleo knew that she couldn't have gone to the beach with Emma and Rikki. *I can't swim! Don't they get it?* She felt hurt that Emma had just allowed Rikki to keep badgering her. Rikki was new, but Emma was her best friend. She *knew* how embarrassed Cleo was about not being able to swim.

At first she waited by the window, hoping that the girls would soon come back and say that nothing weird had happened and everything was back to normal. But the minutes ticked by and there was no sign of them. Cleo moped around the house, picking up things and putting them down, willing time to pass more quickly.

Where are they? she asked herself every few minutes.

After an hour had dragged by, Cleo couldn't stand the suspense any more. She decided to walk over to the Juice-Net Café – the walk would give her something to do and she was bound to see someone she knew. Right now Cleo would be grateful for anything that took her mind off mermaids.

The café was filled with the usual hustle and bustle. A couple of girls were poring over a fashion magazine in the corner, and Cleo glanced their way as she walked in, but she didn't know them. Some boys she knew were playing pool in the middle of the room, but she didn't want to join them. She cheered up when she saw Lewis sitting at one of the internet terminals, but then her heart sank when she looked at the screen.

Lewis was scrolling down a page that was filled with old-fashioned pictures of mermaids and mermen. There were reproductions of

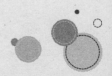

ancient ink drawings – weird-looking creatures with fish tails and inhuman faces. Some of them had frog-like legs emerging from their tails and strange, pointed ears. One seemed to have whiskers like a cat. Another looked like a giant serpent. Cleo felt her flesh creep.

She walked swiftly over to the internet bank. Lewis was so intent on his research that he didn't notice Cleo until she was right behind him. She leaned down and hissed into his ear.

"Lewis, what are you doing?" she asked.

Lewis nearly jumped out of his skin. He looked up at her and she stared back, wondering whether he had guessed something was up.

"Oh, well, you asked," said Lewis, shrugging his shoulders, "so, I dunno, I thought I'd just do some research."

Cleo was not sure whether she felt worried or annoyed. She didn't think he'd have remembered or cared about their earlier conversation. *Uh-oh, perhaps I shouldn't have*

mentioned anything, she thought. She knew how angry Emma and Rikki would be if they found out. She knew that she was going to have to choose her words really carefully.

Lewis glanced sideways at her quickly, then put on his glasses and looked closely at the screen. Cleo didn't notice – she was looking around the café. No one seemed to be paying any attention to what Lewis McCartney was doing, thank goodness.

"That's really nice Lewis," Cleo said eventually. "It's just ... you didn't *need* to do that."

"I know," he said with a little laugh. "But I've got *way* too much time on my hands. Hey, look, I found this really cool stuff ..."

Cleo sighed. She knew that she really didn't have any right to be annoyed with him, but did he *have* to be so helpful all the time? Sometimes it seemed as if she only had to *think* of something and he'd be researching it on the internet for her. *But I guess that's what makes*

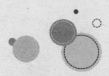

him such a great friend, she realized. *He's always there whenever I need him*. Now that Lewis had done all this research, there was no point ignoring it – she might find out something. Maybe this sort of thing happened all the time ... *although I seriously doubt that*, she told herself.

She smiled at Lewis and suggested that they go for a walk. The café was getting busier because it was coming up to lunchtime, and she didn't want everyone else in the place to hear *this* conversation.

Lewis and Cleo walked out of the café and crossed over to the park. She listened closely as he told her about all the information he had found online. There were tons of cool websites packed with stories, articles and pictures. Lewis had been fascinated by all the legends and theories, and Cleo felt some of his enthusiasm rubbing off on her.

"Mermaid myths have been around for at least 3,000 years," Lewis informed her as they

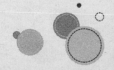

crossed a bridge over one of the canals that cut through the park.

"And people really believed in that stuff?" Cleo asked.

"Yeah, apparently," said Lewis.

Cleo was amazed – if someone had asked her 24 hours ago if there could possibly be any such things as mermaids, she would have laughed in their face. Even now it was hard enough to believe! It seemed as if years ago, people had been much more open to 'extreme possibilities' than they were now.

"Sometimes they were good omens," Lewis was continuing, sounding like some kind of walking encyclopedia. "Sometimes they brought trouble with them."

"What kind of trouble?" Cleo asked, with a growing sense of dread.

But she never got to hear Lewis's answer. Just as she said the word 'trouble', Zane Bennett tore around the corner in front of them

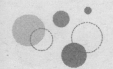

on his dirt bike.

"Oh no," said Cleo, feeling her heart descend rapidly into the pit of her stomach. This was all they needed.

Zane screeched to a halt, blocking their path. Cleo tensed and edged a little closer to Lewis, who looked just as worried as she felt.

"Just ignore him," said Lewis, glaring at Zane and shaking his head.

Lewis despised Zane, who seemed to like nothing better than making other people's lives a misery. Was he picking on Cleo now? Lewis didn't know anything about Cleo's adventures of the night before.

Zane flicked up his visor and aimed a furious glare at Cleo. She turned and pulled Lewis by the arm.

"Let's go back," she said, glancing over her shoulder.

They started to walk back towards the bridge, but Zane snapped his visor back down,

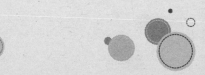

revved his engine and sped straight at them.

"Watch out!" cried Lewis, pushing Cleo off the path and jumping back himself, as Zane did a wheelie between them and skidded to a stop in front of the bridge. "Whoah!"

They had narrowly missed being run over!

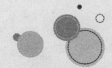

Chapter 14

Zane got off his bike, removed his helmet and turned to face them. His lips were tight with anger. In his black biking gear, he looked really intimidating, and he knew it. Cleo clutched Lewis's arm.

"Nervous?" Zane asked, clearly hoping that the answer was 'yes'.

Cleo let go of Lewis's arm quickly. She didn't want to give Zane the satisfaction of seeing how scared she was.

"What do you want, Zane?" Cleo said.

"My father didn't appreciate having the Water Police knock on his door," Zane spat out, his eyes boring into Cleo's.

"Well, you shouldn't have told me to keep the Zodiac," Cleo answered, amazed at herself for having the courage to speak up. *If I had been*

 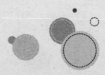

on my own I wouldn't have been able to say a word, she thought. *I'm so glad Lewis is here.*

"I don't like people making me look bad, Cleo," said Zane, moving slowly and deliberately towards them. "*Especially* chicks like you."

He was smiling, but it wasn't a friendly smile. Cleo glanced up at Lewis and then focused on the café in the distance, frowning as she tried to think what to do next. But before she could say another word, Lewis jumped in and took Zane's attention. He had no idea what was going on, but someone had to take the heat off Cleo.

"In front of your dad, you mean, Zane?" Lewis interrupted. "Sounds like you're scared of him."

Lewis seemed perfectly calm. *He's never scared of bullies like Zane*, Cleo thought. She looked around as the boys exchanged insults, wondering how she and Lewis were going to get out of this. If only she could think of something that would just get Zane right out of their way –

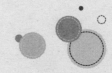

then they could make a run for it.

"You think you're better than me, Lewis, is that it?" Zane asked.

He *was* frightened of his dad, but he didn't want a dork like Lewis to think so.

"Almost everyone's better than you," Lewis snapped back, his light blue eyes locked into Zane's, almost taunting him. "Live with it."

Infuriated, Zane took a few steps forwards. Instantly, Lewis did the same, a frown creasing his forehead.

Cleo's attention was suddenly taken by a red fire hydrant at the side of the path. It felt almost as if it was *demanding* her attention. She couldn't *stop* staring at it. She knew there was water in there, inside the pipes. Cleo knew that this was a dangerous situation and she ought to be taking notice of what the boys were saying, but she couldn't seem to hear them properly. Her ears were buzzing. It was as if the water was singing to her.

"Tough guy?" Zane was saying to Lewis in a mocking tone as they edged closer to one another.

Cleo kept staring at the hydrant. She almost thought that she could *feel* the water inside. That was ridiculous. As if she could *feel* water just by looking at it and wanting it to do something. It was insane! But insane or not, she kept staring, and the hydrant began to tremble.

"Got yourself a protector, have you Cleo?" Zane said, trying to get her attention.

But Cleo wasn't listening. She *could* feel something. And it seemed like the more Zane taunted her and Lewis, the more she felt like doing something to shut him up somehow. A face full of water would do it! *If that hydrant burst ...*

"You and whose army?" Zane sneered. "It's not going to do you any good."

Cleo slowly raised her hand and the hydrant began to shake with the power of the water inside it. Yes! It was happening! The valve on

the hydrant was turning, slowly at first, but then faster as she began to realize that she *was* controlling it. She moved her hand around, sensing that the water inside the hydrant was copying her every move.

"You know, Cleo," said Zane, his expression menacing, "one of these days, with or without Lewis, something really bad might happen to you."

But Cleo wasn't interested in Zane's threats. She somehow knew *exactly* when the water would come surging out of the hydrant. With a surge of joyful power, she felt the valve come off and a torrent of water burst out, directly at Zane's chest.

"Arghh!" cried Zane as the powerful jet of water hit him. It knocked him completely off his feet and he flew backwards through the air, screaming all the way. He landed on his back with a heavy thud and then slid backwards down the muddy slope, rolling straight into the canal. He finally came to a stop in the shallow water,

his expensive bike gear soaked and ruined.

Lewis stared at Zane with his mouth open and Cleo gaped over his shoulder. She could hardly believe what she had just done! She gathered her thoughts and looked back down at the hydrant, which was still shooting out water at top speed. Cleo moved her hand again, in the opposite direction. The water instantly stopped gushing and slowed to a trickle.

Cleo was shocked and a bit scared by what she'd just done. *I controlled water,* she thought, trying to get her head around it. *I actually controlled water!* A smile spread fleetingly across her face. *How awesome!*

Lewis was still staring at Zane, but Cleo knew that any minute now, he would find his voice and turn around to ask her some very awkward questions. *I haven't got time to discuss this*, she thought. *I have to tell Emma and Rikki what happened.* Whatever she had just experienced, she wanted to know if they could do the same. It seemed that the ability to grow

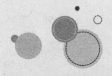

tails wasn't the only thing that had happened to them.

Cleo backed away and ran silently away, down the path and out of sight. By the time Lewis turned around, she had completely disappeared.

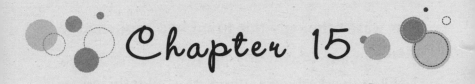

Chapter 15

"So, we climb out of the water and everything's back to normal when we're dry," Emma said to Rikki. "Like nothing ever happened."

"But it did!" said Rikki. "Oh, that's gotta be one of the best experiences of my life. I mean, are there even *words* for that?"

"I don't think so!" said Emma, happily.

They were strolling up to Emma's front door, back in their shorts and vest tops. As soon as they had come out of the water and dried off, their tails had disappeared and it was as if they had never been in the water at all. Even their hair was dry and neatly tied up. They had stayed on the beach for a few minutes, talking eagerly about the amazing time they had had in the sea. Then Emma had jumped to her feet – she had to find Cleo and tell her about everything that had happened to them underwater – and to let her

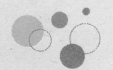

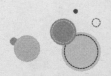

know that it was nothing to be scared of.

They hadn't been able to stop talking about their experiences all the way home. Emma decided that it was like the most awesome dive you could ever imagine, but better than that, because you didn't need oxygen tanks or wetsuits or fancy equipment. She was longing to know how deep and how far they would be able to swim.

Rikki felt as though she was walking on air. She couldn't decide what had been more spectacular – playing tag with a dolphin or using her tail to spin like a drill as she sped along. *I can't wait to get back in the water and find out what else we can do!* she thought.

As they stepped up to Emma's front door, they heard Cleo's voice calling them.

"Wait!" she yelled.

Emma and Rikki turned, and saw Cleo running up the path behind them. She stopped, trying to catch her breath as she had run non-stop all the way from the park. Then she

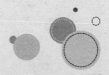

grabbed each of them by the arm.

"You will never *believe* what just happened!" she said, pushing them towards the front door.

More exciting than what we've just done? Rikki said to herself. *I don't think so!*

Emma just stared at Cleo in surprise. What could have got her so excited?

Cleo told them all about what had happened to her that morning. They went upstairs to Emma's bedroom, Cleo talking as fast as she could all the way. Emma and Rikki sat on the bed and Cleo dropped into the desk chair in front of them, waving her arms around to try to paint a picture for her friends of what had happened.

Emma and Rikki looked worried when they heard about Lewis's internet research, but Cleo shushed them. That was nothing! When she described how Zane had cornered her, and how she had been drawn to the fire hydrant, they were doubtful and confused. Cleo stumbled over her words, trying to explain the strange

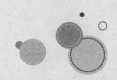

feeling that had come over her, how she felt she could control the water just by *thinking* about it. But even as she was talking she knew that it sounded weird and very, *very* unlikely. Emma and Rikki wcrc wearing identical expressions – somewhere between bewilderment and concern.

They think I'm crazy, Cleo said to herself. *I'll just have to show them!* She jumped up and raced out of the room.

Emma and Rikki exchanged glances.

It's not like Cleo to completely make something up, Emma thought, *but she does let her imagination run away with her sometimes. Does she really mean that she can control water?*

This would be awesome, if it's true, Rikki was thinking. *But I've never heard any stories about mermaids controlling the water. In fairy tales they're always just swimming about in the ocean, falling in love with humans!*

Rikki grinned at this thought and Emma looked curious, but before she could speak Cleo burst back into the room with a glass of water

from the kitchen. She slammed the bedroom door shut, plonked the glass of water on the desk and sat down in her chair again.

Now they'll see what I mean, she thought, raising her hand and moving it as she had next to the fire hydrant. For a moment, nothing happened. Cleo gritted her teeth. She really wanted to amaze Rikki and Emma with a stunning display of her new-found powers. She felt like a magician or something! She concentrated *really* hard. Then she began to feel the water again, just as she had in the park. Somehow she could sense exactly what it was going to do – she could feel and control each tiny molecule.

The water started to tremble. Then, slowly and waveringly, it spiralled up out of the glass in a thin, transparent column. Cleo frowned as she focused on the water, her right hand stretched out towards the glass while her left hand lay in her lap. Emma and Rikki sat in stunned silence, gazing up at the water as their friend

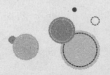

concentrated on controlling it. It was beautiful … and impossible.

"And it grows even more," Cleo told them as the column grew taller.

It rose higher and higher, until it almost touched the ceiling. More and more water poured upwards from the glass to form a long, twisting rope of flowing liquid that was totally under Cleo's command.

"Where's the extra water coming from?" asked Rikki, finally finding her voice.

There was far more liquid in the column than the glass could possibly have held.

"I don't know …" Cleo shrugged, waving her arm out towards her friends and breaking her concentration.

With Cleo's movement, the water column toppled sharply towards Rikki and Emma. Rikki turned her face away, bracing herself for the cold water. Acting on instinct, Emma threw up her hands in front of her for protection and

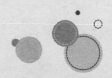

threw herself back. But there was no drenching – no cold splash. The instant that Emma held up her hands, there was a cold crackle and the water froze like a thin, curving ice sculpture, arching over Emma's bed.

The three girls froze for a moment too – in disbelief. Cleo's mouth dropped open.

"Did I do that?" Emma asked, sitting back up.

"It wasn't *me*," Cleo replied.

"Okay," said Rikki, looking first at Emma and then at Cleo, "this is over the top. I'm getting tingles now."

She gave a half smile, almost as if she expected one of them to admit that it was all one big, elaborate trick.

Emma thought back over what had just happened.

"All I did was …" she said, thrusting out her hand with her palm facing out. This time she aimed it at a vase on the windowsill. The water

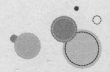

inside it froze instantly.

The three girls exchanged smiles. This was awesome!

I wonder what my power is, thought Rikki.

Cleo and Emma were wondering the same thing. Cleo was relieved that she had been able to show them what she could do, and stunned that Emma had this magical power too. So if she could control water's movements, and Emma could freeze water, what could Rikki do?

There's only one way to find out! Rikki said to herself.

She concentrated on the column of water that Emma had just frozen and flung her hands out towards it. Nothing. She tried positioning her hands differently, making different shapes with her fingers. It just sat there, frozen in place over the bed.

"*Not fair!*" Rikki wailed. "Why don't I get to do the cool stuff?"

"I don't think 'cool' is the word. It's *scary*,"

Cleo said.

Rikki shook her head. *Cleo's sweet, but way too cautious,* she thought. *This isn't scary – this is fantastic! If only I had some sort of power too …*

"But you should've seen the *look* on Zane's face," Cleo continued, with a sudden flash of mischief. Rikki giggled with her.

"This isn't funny," Emma told them. Her face was solemn. "We've gotta keep this a secret – from everyone. We could end up dissected, or in the circus or something."

Rikki stopped giggling. She knew that Emma was right.

"So, this secret – it's just between the three of us?" asked Cleo, who *loved* secrets.

"Our secret," said Emma, nodding and looking first at Rikki and then at Cleo. "Our responsibility. Whatever happens, we're in this together."

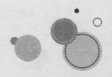

No one knew what to say. Cleo knew Emma was serious, but she'd never seen her *this* serious. Rikki looked at her two new friends, pleased that they had a pact, but feeling the need to break the silence with a joke.

"It doesn't mean we're married does it?" she asked.

Cleo half smiled and then bit it back, expecting Emma to yell at Rikki for being flippant. But Emma understood Rikki's humour a lot better now. *I guess I can be a bit too serious sometimes*, she thought. *It's good to have someone around to lighten up the atmosphere.*

"Now that was actually *funny!*" she said with a smile.

The three of them grinned at each other. They were linked by an unbreakable bond now – three best friends, sharing a common secret. It was just like Emma had said: whatever happened next, they were in this together.

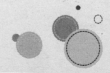